Nowhere To Go!

Adapted by
Benjamin Hulme-Cross

One day, some men were running after Donkey in the forest.

Suddenly, Donkey crashed into something big and green.
It was Shrek! The men ran away.

"What are you?" asked Shrek. "Go away!"

"I am a donkey. I am all alone,"
said Donkey. He followed Shrek.

"Why are you following me?" asked Shrek.
"I'm an ogre!"

"You *are* very big and green ..." said Donkey.
"You should be frightened of me!" Shrek cried.

"I'm not frightened of you," said Donkey.

Donkey followed Shrek deeper into the forest.

They came to a swamp. In the swamp
there was a little muddy house.

"Yuck!" said Donkey. "Who would live in a smelly swamp?"

"Me! That's my home!" said Shrek.

"Oh," said Donkey. "Well … can I stay with you?"

"No!" yelled Shrek.

"Please!" cried Donkey. "I have nowhere to go!"

Shrek felt sorry for Donkey.

"OK," said Shrek. "You can stay for one night ...

… outside!"